Covens and Curses

PREQUEL NOVELLA

NOT ALL WITCHES LIVE IN SALEM

SELENE ARNOLD

COVENS AND CURSES
By Selene Arnold
Series: NOT ALL WITCHES LIVE IN SALEM
Prequel Novella

This is a work of fiction. Names, characters, places, and incidents are
products of the author's imagination or are used fictitiously and are not to
be construed as real. Any resemblance to actual events, locales,
organizations, or persons, living or dead, is entirely coincidental.

Cover Art: Rebecca Frank, Bewitching Book Covers
(www.rebeccafrank.design).

ISBN 979-8-9869722-3-7 (pbk)
ISBN 979-8-9869722-4-4 (ebook)

First paperback edition, 2023
MOON MAGICK PUBLICATIONS LLC
www.selenearnold.com

For all the women in my life,
but especially my daughter.

Do not fear the witches,
Fear the ones that burn them.
We must rise together,
Grab your besoms, tonight we ride.

Chapter One

T he village council of Montclair had already claimed
thirteen innocent souls this moon cycle. Madeleine
Dubois would soon be the fourteenth.

Their hearts were heavy as the eerie silence filled the
room. Margot, Eloise, and Amelie, Madeleine's daughters,
huddled close together, holding hands. A mixture of fear and
disbelief, as the sisters sat in their cottage, in the small French
town of Montclair. The distant murmurs of the townspeople
broke the silence. They did their best to honor their mother's
wishes. She had prepared them for this day; they had been
preparing their entire lives.

Margot, the eldest sister with fiery red hair and a determined gaze, glanced out the window, her hands trembling.
She could see their mother, Madeleine, standing in the village
square, surrounded by an angry mob. The air was thick with
accusation, and the scent of burning torches filled their
nostrils.

Eloise, the middle sister, with soft brown curls cascading down her back, reached out and grasped Margot's trembling hand. Her hazel eyes welled up with tears, glistening like dewdrops. She couldn't bear the thought of their mother being subjected to such cruelty.

Amelie, the youngest sister, her raven-black hair framing her delicate porcelain face, got up and paced anxiously across the room. Her mind raced, searching for a way to protect their mother from the impending trial. She couldn't fathom how the village could accuse their peaceful, loving mother of such heinous crimes.

"We have to do something," Margot whispered. "We can't let them condemn her without a fight."

Eloise nodded, her voice quivering. "We know Mother is innocent. We've seen her help so many. She is a healer, not the monster they are making her out to be. She would never hurt someone outside of protecting us."

Amelie's eyes sparkled with a glimmer of hope. "Perhaps we can gather evidence to prove her innocence. We need to find witnesses who can testify on her behalf."

Margot sighed loudly. "Mother knew that this day would come. She knew our way of life could bring unnecessary attention. That is why she showed us how to be careful; she had a plan if they ever accused her. It's almost as if she knew exactly what was going to happen."

The sisters exchanged a resolute nod, their bond strong. They knew they faced a daunting task, but they were deter-mined to save their mother. The townspeople had made a spectacle of the witch trials.

As the sun dipped below the horizon, casting the village into darkness, the sisters dispersed, each on their own mission. Margot went to find the books hidden in their family cottage, determined to uncover any information that might shed light on the truth. Eloise ventured into the bustling marketplace, seeking whispers and hints of doubt among the villagers. Amelie, with her quick wit and persuasive charm, roamed the streets, listening for any signs of hidden motives behind the accusations. Their plan was simple, they just needed to execute.

Margot engulfed herself in ancient tomes, searching for any evidence that would debunk the claims of cruelty against their mother.

Eloise engaged in heartfelt conversations with the towns-people. She did her best to remind them of all the ways her mother had helped each of them individually. She planted seeds of doubt in their minds, hoping to sway public opinion.

Amelie, with her keen intuition, collected stories and rumors that hinted at ulterior motives behind the accusations.

One by one, the pieces of their puzzle fit together. Margot discovered faded manuscripts that spoke of natural remedies and herbal cures. She compiled a list of examples in which their mother helped people of the town. Eloise, through her gentle persuasion, found townspeople who secretly doubted their mother's guilt. She held their whispers of support like fragile wings of hope. Amelie unraveled the threads of jealousy and revenge, weaving a tapestry of motives that fueled the accusations.

With their evidence in hand, the sisters reconvened in their candle-lit living room. Their faces were weary but reso-lute. They bore the weight of their relentless pursuit of justice. Their father had not left their mother's side. He spent every moment outside her cell, not sleeping for one second.

"We cannot wait any longer," Margot declared. "Tomorrow is the trial, and we must present our evidence to the judge and rally those who doubt. There are enough examples of ways she healed and helped each of the families in this town."

Eloise nodded, a flicker of hope igniting in her eyes. "We will fight for Mother's freedom. We won't let them take her away from us."

Amelie spoke. "Together, we are strong. Our bond as sisters will be our greatest weapon. Mother has always emphasized that our individual abilities were nothing compared to the three of us together."

In that moment, their unity solidified, and a surge of determination coursed through their veins. They clasped hands, forming a circle, their love and determination intertwining. Soon a bright white light radiating from the middle of their small circle.

"Protect her," they chanted in unison, as the light began to grow and surround them.

The morning air was thick with tension as Margot, Eloise, and Amelie stood in the crowded village square. They were bound by love and an unyielding determination, but the trial had begun, and their mother, Madeleine, was at the center. They clung to each other, their hearts pounding, as they watched the events unfold before them.

Madeleine stood tall, her face serene and calm. The villagers continued to hurl ridiculous accusations at her. The judge, Lord of De Lancre, a stern man with a long gray beard, read aloud.

"Heart, she has none, not even for the men she loved." The villagers, fueled by fear and superstition, jeered and spat at her, their eyes filled with hatred.

"Madeleine Dubois, you stand accused of thirteen deaths, the illness of four children, the failure of our village's crops, and the dysfunction of multiple councilmen."

It's all a lie, Margot thought to herself. Her grip tightening around her sisters' hands as their father, Henri, stepped forward, his voice trembling with defiance.

"I implore you, good people, to see reason," Henri pleaded, his voice carrying over the crowd. "My wife is innocent, only a compassionate spirit—she has committed no crimes."

The judge's eyes narrowed, his gaze cold and unyielding. "Your words hold no weight, Henri. We have seen the signs, the strange occurrences that surround your wife. She is a witch, and she must be punished."

A gasp rippled through the crowd, and Margot felt her heart drop. She exchanged a glance with Eloise and Amelie, their eyes filled with sorrow and fear.

Suddenly, chaos erupted as Henri lunged forward, driven by desperation and love. He had spent the last two days outside the cell wall. Trying to reassure Madeleine that he wouldn't leave her—even though she begged him to leave town with their daughters. He fought his way through the villagers, his determined strides leading him to Madeleine's side. The sisters watched in horror as their father, a strong and proud man, tried to shield their mother from harm.

But the mob was relentless, fueled by their collective fear and anger. They descended upon Henri, their blows raining down upon him. His blood spilled at Madeleine's feet, tears flooding her face. Margot wanted to scream, to rush to their father's aid, but she was frozen in place, paralyzed by the brutality unfolding before her.

Amidst the chaos, Madeleine's eyes locked with her

daughters', a silent plea for them to stay strong. Her voice, barely a whisper, reached their ears.

"You must go, my loves. My love will always be yours. No matter what happens, hold on to that love."

Tears streamed down Margot's face as she watched her father's lifeless body being dragged away. The judge, unmoved by the surrounding chaos, declared the sentence, sealing Madeleine's destiny. They stripped her naked and bound her hands as they forced water down her throat. First, they would use water torture, and then, depending on the appetite of the villagers, it might progress to hanging. Considering the anger in their eyes, it was likely she would burn at the stake.

Before they witnessed too much, Margot led the sisters inconspicuously out of the town square. With tear-stained faces and broken hearts, they found solace in each other's embrace. They clung to one another, their tears mingling with the pain that swelled in their hearts.

In the night's darkness, surrounded by the shadows of loss, Margot, Eloise, and Amelie remained in the shadows. With hearts heavy but minds resolute, the sisters clung to the love that bound them together. It was their beacon of hope, their guiding star in a world filled with cruelty and despair. They knew the road ahead would be treacherous, but they would face it together, armed with the love that had defined their family.

Quiet and thoughtful, Amelie made herself another vow. Her intuition had guided her to very specific families in the town. There had been accusations from one family in particular that seemed more personal than superstitious. Almost as if an old lover made her pay for his broken heart. Amelie didn't know exactly, but her intuition had never failed her before and she was determined to find out the truth.

They had lost their mother, their guiding light, and now their father, a hero who had fought for love until his last breath. Today, they had lost the battle, but they wouldn't let evil win the war. Somehow, they would protect the innocent. The death of their parents would not be in vain.

Chapter Two

The moon hung high in the ink-black sky, casting an ethereal glow upon the village. Margot, Eloise, and Amelie, moved swiftly through the narrow cobblestone streets. Their footsteps muffled and breaths hushed as they navigated the familiar paths toward the outskirts of town. Few would venture into the darkened woods on this full moon. Thankfully, the superstitions of the town would keep them away. They only needed to make it into the darkened woods without being spotted.

The events of the past days had left the sisters shattered, their hearts heavy with the loss of their parents, who had paid the ultimate price for their love. The witch trials had claimed their lives, leaving the sisters with no choice but to flee, to escape the clutches of a town poisoned by fear and prejudice. They took only the supplies that they could carry. The most important was their mother's potions, family heirloom jewels and their family's book of shadows and light.

Margot led the way, her senses sharp and alert. She had always been resourceful, and now she relied on those skills to guide them to safety. Eloise, her hazel eyes full of emotion, followed closely behind, her steps steady. Amelie's spirit, undeterred, brought up the rear, her senses keen and her mind sharp.

As they neared the edge of the village, the sisters quickened their pace, their hearts pounding in their chests, their hooded cloaks hiding their faces. They knew that their departure must be swift, for the night offered them a fleeting veil of darkness and secrecy.

The darkened woods loomed before Margot, Eloise, and Amelie. Its ancient trees whispering secrets as the sisters ventured deeper into its depths. An unexplainable pull guided them. Their hearts filled with anticipation and curiosity as they followed an overgrown path that seemed to beckon them forward.

As they ventured further, the forest grew denser; the moonlight filtering through the thick canopy above, casting ethereal patterns on the forest floor. It filled the air with the scent of moss and damp earth, as if the forest itself held its breath, guarding the secret that lay ahead.

It felt like hours, but eventually they reached a small, abandoned cottage. It was nestled amidst a grove of ancient trees. Margot motioned for her sisters to enter.

As they stepped inside, a sense of warmth and belonging that seemed to hang in the air greeted the sisters. Soft rays of sunlight filtered through the cracked windows, casting a golden glow on the worn wooden floorboards.

The air inside was musty, the remnants of past lives long forgotten. It was not much, but it would provide them with a temporary refuge.

Time had worn away at its walls, and ivy crawled over its

weathered exterior. Yet, there was an undeniable charm that emanated from the hidden haven.

"This place feels... familiar," Eloise whispered, her voice filled with awe as she traced her fingers along the faded wallpaper. "As if it has been waiting for us."

Margot and Amelie exchanged knowing glances, their hearts filled with a mixture of wonder and realization. There was a sense of destiny that settled upon them, as if this hidden cottage had been destined to be discovered by their hands.

Exploring further, they discovered a quaint sitting area adorned with tattered cushions, a fireplace where flames had long since died out, and a small kitchen that held remnants of a life that had once thrived.

"This place has been untouched by time," Amelie mused, her voice filled with reverence. "It's as if it has been preserved, waiting for us to find it."

Margot nodded, a glimmer of excitement in her eyes. "Mother and Father's spirits are with us."

And so, the sisters set to work, clearing away the dust and breathing life back into the hidden cottage. They repaired the broken windows, tended to the neglected garden, and transformed the forgotten space into a sanctuary of hope and resistance.

In the dim light, the sisters gathered around a rickety wooden table, their faces illuminated by the flickering candlelight. Amelie's voice trembled as she spoke, her words laden with determination.

"We cannot let them get away with this," she whispered, her voice filled with conviction. "Someone did this to mother and knew that father would follow her to the grave."

Margot nodded, her fiery gaze meeting her sisters' eyes. "We have seen the darkness that lives within this town, the ignorance and fear that has taken hold. We must not let it consume us. Our path lies beyond these borders."

Eloise, her voice unwavering, spoke next. "We must find allies, those who believe in justice and will stand against the tyranny of these trials. Together, we will gather strength and expose the truth."

Amelie burst out in anger, tears falling down her face. "Someone did this to them. I am telling you, sisters, someone did this to them and we will be next. We must figure it out before it's too late. I cannot lose you as well."

Margot rushed to her sister's side and held her close. Eloise quickly followed. It was Margot's job now to watch over and care for her sisters. The sisters locked hands, their fingers intertwining.

Margot and Amelie watched as Eloise slouched, her body exhausted from the recent tragedy filled days. Without even thinking, Margot reached out and caught her sister before she fell to the ground. Margot and Amelie's eyes met with concern.

"Ellie, you must rest," Margot demanded, as she helped her sister lay down. Her bright pink cheeks and pale skin gave Margot a quickening in her gut. The world around her paused as an image posed in the forefront of her mind.

No, it isn't possible.

Margot took another look at her sister resting peacefully and decided it wasn't the time to ask.

Chapter Three

The small, abandoned cottage stood as a silent witness to the sisters' discussions, their voices echoing through the dimly lit room. Margot, Eloise, and Amelie sat around the worn wooden table, their expressions reflecting the weight of their decisions.

Amidst the heavy silence, Eloise's voice broke through. "I understand the need to leave, to seek allies and start new where no one could recognize us," she began, her voice steady. "But I cannot bear the thought of abandoning our village completely, of leaving behind the memories of our parents… Montclair is our home."

Margot's eyebrows furrowed, her fiery gaze meeting Eloise's. "But, sister, staying near this village puts us at risk. The witch trials have poisoned the minds of the villagers. It's dangerous for us to remain here. You saw what they did to mother."

Eloise's voice remained resolute as she responded, her

hands clenched tightly. "I know the risks, Margot, but I cannot bear the guilt of abandoning our home and others we care about. I want to stay and help protect them, to be a beacon of hope in this darkness."

Amelie interjected. "Perhaps there is a way we can honor both paths. Eloise could stay close to our village, protecting our home and gathering support, while Margot and I venture further to seek allies and resources."

"Are there any members of the coven still alive?" Eloise asked, looking at her big sister, Margot.

"No, they were all killed. If any of their family members lived, they wouldn't want anything to do with us. It would just bring them unnecessary attention and remind them of the pain." Margot said, quickly. She wanted to ignore the thoughts.

A glimmer of hope danced in Eloise's eyes as she considered Amelie's words, ignoring Margot's thoughts about the coven. She hadn't yet acknowledged her fainting spell and knew her exhaustion had worried Margot. "Yes, that could work. Margot, you and Amelie can travel to other villages, find those who share support. Meanwhile, I will stay here, working from within, rallying support and protecting those in need."

Margot sighed, her fierce determination momentarily softened. "I worry about your safety, Eloise. These times are dangerous, and the risks are great." Her eyes soft with concern, "You need more rest than you imagine, sister. If I am not with you, how can I be sure you are safe?"

Eloise reached out and placed a reassuring hand on Margot's. "Trust in me, dear sister. I won't take unnecessary risks, and I'll be cautious. My heart tells me this is the path I must take." She hoped her sisters wouldn't see the real reason she wanted to stay.

Amelie, always the mediator, smiled softly. "It seems we have found a solution to honor our different desires. Together, we will fight against the darkness, each in our own way."

It had been weeks since their parent's deaths, but it was still not safe. The sisters set their plans into motion. Margot and Amelie bid farewell to Eloise, feeling a mixture of worry and hope. Eloise watched her sisters depart, her determination unwavering. She knew their eldest sister would protect Amelie. Margot had always been like a second mother to them. After all, there were five years between them. Mother had suffered many miscarriages after the birth of Margot, and she was terrified of never having other children. Margot begged for sisters. It explained the extra patience she always showed them.

In the days and nights that followed, Eloise worked tirelessly, her actions driven by a deep-rooted love for her village and the people who dwelled within it. As often as she thought of Margot and Amelie, she reminded herself to rest as much as possible. She had been getting flushed and light-headed often, so she searched in the darkened woods for a remedy. Her mother would always make a drink of chamomile and ginger. She missed her and could hardly spend a moment thinking about her without crying.

Margot and Amelie had always been close, but were the farthest apart in age. They both worried about Eloise for different reasons. They were careful to only travel by night and to wear their cloaks to hide their faces. But neither of them could deny their concern for their sister, who was back at their home without them.

"Do you think we should go back to check on Ellie?" Amelie asked with hopeful eyes.

Margot had been fighting the urge to return and do just that. She hadn't wanted to acknowledge that she had made the wrong choice of leaving. In the nights that followed their departure, her mother had come to her in her dreams often. Telling her she should be with her sister, but Margot was battling herself. In her heart and mind, there was a constant fight for her next steps. She had always followed her intuition, which often came in the voice of her mother, but her emotions made everything muddy. She didn't know if it was fear or guilt, or if Eloise might think she didn't trust her.

"Margot?" Amelie repeated. She hoped to snap her sister out of her daydream. "Margot!" She whispered aggressively as she grasped her sister by the arm and pulled her back. There was someone in the clearing ahead, but luckily, they hadn't noticed them yet.

The sisters ducked behind a large gathering of trees at the edge of the darkened woods, watching the figure in the clearing. He turned in their direction, and Margot's hand covered Amelie's mouth in the moment she gasped. They had both clearly recognized him. Something distracted him at that moment as a hawk in the sky swooped in his direction.

"We must get back to Ellie at once," Margot muttered as she pulled her sister in the other direction.

Chapter Four

Eloise stood alone in the quiet sanctuary of the moonlit forest, her hand gently cradling her abdomen. A mix of emotions swirled within her, blending joy and trepidation into a fragile balance. Her heart knew the truth before her mind had fully grasped it—she was with child.

The realization filled her with a profound sense of awe and wonder, but it also brought forth a wave of uncertainty. Eloise had been so consumed by her grief and so focused on protecting her home from dangers that the possibility of motherhood had seemed a distant dream. And yet, life had blossomed amid their tumultuous journey.

Oh, my little one. I will make this world better for you. As she stood there, lost in her thoughts, Eloise felt a presence behind her. The butterflies filled her stomach as she felt the warm energy and love radiating from behind her. She turned to find Margot and Amelie, their expressions of concern and anticipation difficult to hide.

Margot's eyes sparkled with a mix of emotions. "Ellie, I sensed it," she whispered, her voice filled with tenderness. "I have felt the whispers of new life surrounding you, the delicate thread that connects us all."

Amelie stepped forward, her voice soft and reassuring. "You don't have to face this alone, dear sister. We are here for you, every step of the way." Finally realizing why her mother had come to her in her dreams, urging her to be with her sister. She had felt a new energy within her sister, but hadn't understood it completely.

Eloise's breath caught in her throat as she absorbed their words. In that moment, she realized her sisters had sensed the life growing within her before she had even spoken a word. The bond that had always united them had transcended mere words and gestures—it had become an unspoken language of love and understanding.

Tears welled in Eloise's eyes as she reached out to embrace her sisters, their arms wrapping around her in a warm and comforting embrace. In that moment, she felt the weight of her worries and uncertainties lifted, replaced by a profound sense of gratitude and love.

"I am grateful to have you by my side," Eloise said, her voice filled with emotion. "To know that I don't have to face this journey alone brings me strength and reassurance."

Margot smiled, her voice filled with unwavering support. "We are a family, Ellie. We face everything together, the joys and the challenges. Your child will be surrounded by love and a legacy of resilience that will guide them through life."

Amelie nodded, her eyes shining with determination. She glanced at Margot, wondering if she was going to tell Ellie about the man in the clearing. Margot shook her head, squeezing both sisters harder.

Eloise sat by the window of the cottage, her gaze lost in the distance. The warmth of the hearth enveloped her, but her heart felt heavy with a mix of excitement and fear. It was unbelievable that she was carrying a precious life within her, a piece of her, and the love that had once brought her both happiness and pain.

As she caressed her slowly growing belly, memories of a conversation with her mother resurfaced like whispers from the past. She remembered the tender moments they had shared, her mother's voice filled with love and concern.

"Love can be a beautiful and powerful force, my dear Eloise," her mother had said, her eyes filled with wisdom, but also a spark of worry. "But it can also blind us to the truth, to the intentions of those who may not have our best interests at heart. Guard your heart, my sweet girl, and remember that true love should never come at the expense of your own well-being."

Eloise had listened to her mother's words, but she had been swept away by the intoxicating emotions that love had ignited within her. Now, as she carried a life within her, she understood the weight of her mother's words more deeply than ever before.

Tears welled in Eloise's eyes as she whispered to the life growing inside her. "I will protect you with all that I am, my little one. I will learn from the mistakes of my past and shield you from any pain that may come your way."

In that moment, a sense of strength washed over her. She knew her journey was not just about protecting her sisters, but also about creating a safe and nurturing environment for her child.

Eloise joined her sisters in the cottage's heart. Their eyes met, and with no words, they understood the depths of Eloise's emotions.

"So, who is the father?" Amelie asked without warning. She had been dying to ask from the moment she realized her sister was pregnant. Her sisters had always attempted to keep her sheltered from their personal escapades. It wasn't uncommon for them to sneak off in the middle of the night, or during a celebration in the darkened woods. But She had never expected this. Boys were the last thing on Amelie's mind. The room was silent and the sisters just stared, waiting for the others to respond.

Margot was the first to break the silence. "Ellie, you can tell us. What are you afraid of?" She held out both of her hands, gesturing for her sisters to take them.

"You hate him." Eloise mumbled under her breath.

"NO! Ellie," Margot responded quickly, as she shook. "You know you can't trust him and he's too old for you." She hardly ever lost her composure, but in this moment, she couldn't hold back. She dropped her sister's hands, sat back in her chair, and cried.

"Would one of you please fill me in?" Amelie asked calmly.

"This is why you've been keeping it a secret." Margot whispered accusingly as her crying slowed.

"I didn't mean for it to happen." Eloise cried. "It started by accident, but then I couldn't stop myself. I should've thought of you and how he broke your heart, but he had me convinced that we were different."

Amelie's wide hazel eyes looked back and forth between her sisters. She tried to gather the bits and pieces since neither of them was going to explain. From the moment they all knew that Ellie was to have a child, there was nothing but joy and excitement. It had been a breath of fresh air since the death of their parents.

"Let's get some rest. We can talk more in the morning." Amelie urged both of them. She closed her eyes and envisioned the white light of joy that her mother had used many times to calm them as children. It began in her core and radiated outward. Soon it enveloped all three of them and her sister's emotions slowed. She took in a deep breath, and they followed. She exhaled slowly, and they did the same. After a few moments, the light dissipated and the energy in the room was calm. Margot and Eloise reached for each other and hugged.

"If you love him and he loves you, then I am happy for you. I just don't trust him," Margot whispered.

"I do," Eloise said with glistening eyes.

Their mother had taught Amelie how to channel calming energy as a little girl. Often Amelie had strong, complex emotions without the ability to communicate them in words. This practice had saved her many times over the years, but it was the first time she had ever had to use it on both of her sisters at once.

She recalled the first time she used it to help Margot, after she found the object of her affection wrapped up in another girl. It was at that moment that it occurred to her who her sisters were talking about.

Chapter Five

The moon hung high in the night sky, casting a silver glow upon the hidden cottage and the slumbering sisters. Eloise lay in her bed, heart pounding with both excitement and anxiety. Her decision had been made; tonight, she would venture out into the night to find her love and share the news of their growing child.

As the soft snores of her sisters filled the room, Eloise slipped out of bed, careful not to disturb their peaceful sleep. She dressed in silence, her movements graceful and calculated. Each step was filled with purpose, driven by a love that burned within her. She knew the risks involved, but the desire to share this moment with her beloved was too strong to ignore.

With a last glance at her sisters, Eloise crept towards the door, her heart pounding in her chest. She opened it with the utmost care, wincing as it creaked ever so lightly. She held her breath, hoping her departure had gone unnoticed.

The dark forest greeted her with an embrace, its ancient trees whispering secrets as she ventured deeper into its depths. Her senses heightened, every rustle of leaves and the close hoot of an owl echoing in her ears. The physical path she followed was new, but the gravitational pull toward him had been etched into her memory from countless clandestine meetings.

As she approached the clearing where they had often met, her heart swelled with anticipation. She longed to see the joy in his eyes, to share the news that would forever change their lives. Then, all at once, fear brought her down to the reality of the world around them. *Is he going to be happy? Will he be scared? This wasn't something that she ever expected.* But just as she stepped into the clearing, a voice cut through the silence, freezing her in her tracks.

"Eloise," the voice boomed, filled with authority and disapproval. "What are you doing out here at this hour?"

Eloise's heart sank as she turned to face the stern figure emerging from the shadows. It was her love's father, a man known for his strict adherence to tradition and his disdain for their forbidden love. She braced herself, her voice trembling but filled with determination.

"I... I came to speak with your son," Eloise stammered, her eyes meeting his with fear and defiance. "I have something important to tell him."

His eyes narrowed, a mix of anger and disappointment clear in his gaze. "You dare to defy me and sneak out in the dead of night? What could be so important that it couldn't wait until morning?"

Eloise took a deep breath. This was not how she wanted him to find out. She imagined a beautiful moment of privacy between the two of them. She refused to tell his father, the man who forbid their love.

"You and your sisters haven't been seen in town, since we exposed your mother for her heinous ways. Where have you been hiding?" He asked, getting too close for her comfort.

"We've been grieving. My mother was innocent of the crimes they accused her of, so the experience was quite traumatic. My sisters and I need time." She explained. She refused to tell him any more than that.

As they stood there silent in the dark, the moon peeked out from the clouds and there was a dark red hue to it. At that moment, Eloise knew she was in danger. There was blood on the moon. Mother always described the red hues as beautiful and dangerous all at once. Shivers climbed up her spine, and she did her best to stay in the moment. In the corner of her eye, she saw movement and before she could turn around; he grabbed her by the arms.

"You're coming back with us," He whispered. "It would be best if you didn't fight it."

Us? She thought as she looked in his eyes. Fear overcame her, and she tried to pull away. The more she pulled, the harder he gripped her. Until she felt someone grab her wrists from behind, holding them in one hand while quickly covering her mouth with the other. The unidentified man kept his face out of view and an eerie feeling came over her.

As Eloise followed them back towards their village, her mind spun with uncertainty. She had taken a risk, one that could have dire consequences, but she believed it was a risk worth taking—for her child. Now she wasn't so sure.

Chapter Six

Francois felt nothing but guilt as he laid in bed that night. All he could do was think back to the night before when he accompanied his father to the councilmen's meeting.

He remembered the whispers of fear and distrust that filled the air as the town's leaders gathered in secrecy. The Dubois sisters' efforts to expose the injustices had not gone unnoticed. They saw an opportunity in Eloise, the sister who had a forbidden affair with Lord de Clarmont's son. They were the most established family in the town, and she did not follow the warnings to leave him alone. Now they would exploit her.

"These sisters pose a threat to our authority," the priest declared, his voice filled with venomous determination. "We must devise a plan to capture them, in order to extinguish the flames of rebellion once and for all."

The room fell into hushed deliberation as the leaders

discussed their options. They threw ideas around, some more ruthless than others. But amidst the chaos, one plan emerged —a dangerous gambit that involved using Eloise as bait to lure her sisters out of hiding.

"We must use Eloise's vulnerability against her," one of the council members suggested, a sinister smile playing on his lips. "We know where they have been meeting secretly and tomorrow, the night of the full moon is time once again. Once we have her in our grasp, her sisters will have no choice but to reveal themselves."

The plan was met with mixed reactions, but the leaders agreed it was their best chance at capturing the sisters and quelling the growing resistance. Their hatred and fear blinded them to the moral implications of their actions, fueling their determination to maintain control at any cost. They knew that Eloise's love for her sisters would be the key to their capture.

The following morning, Francois snuck out into the clearing, deep in the darkened woods, to tie a ribbon on a branch. This was the sign that Louis, his brother, would use to signal to Eloise to meet that night.

Each day, Eloise would take her walk to gather herbs and plants, walking near enough to the clearing to see if Louis could sneak away. That day, she saw the ribbon and her heart fluttered with excitement. She knew the risks involved, but the possibility of seeing him and sharing the news was something she had to do.

As she stepped out of the hidden cottage, the moon cast an ethereal glow upon her, as if the world itself knew of the dangers that awaited. Her footsteps were filled with determination, and tonight would be the night that would decide the future of herself and her unborn child.

Little did she know that the town's leaders watched her every step, their eyes gleaming with a sinister satisfaction.

The trap had been set, and they were confident that they would finally rid themselves of the sisters who dared to challenge their authority.

The cottage stood in an eerie silence as Margot and Amelie awoke with no Eloise. The absence of Eloise weighed upon them like a suffocating fog, leaving a void that threatened to consume their resolve, their hearts heavy with worry. They knew they had to act swiftly to find her, to bring her back safely. There was never any circumstance not to tell the others where she was going.

Margot remembered that many years ago, she would sneak out to at night to find Louis. While the thought of her sister with the man that broke her heart tore through her like ripping flesh, she needed to get past it to find her sister. *The clearing*, she thought.

They made their way to the clearing, cautious and quiet. The sun had only begun to rise when she spotted the ribbon in the tree. The disgust filled her as she realized Louis used the same techniques with her sister, as he did with her many years before. After looking around carefully, they found the many shoe prints in the mud near the center of the clearing. Chills ran up her spine. Without saying a word, Amelie looked at Margot and they knew where their sister was.

They went back to the cottage, devising a plan to rescue their sister. They needed to hide who they were when Amelie suggested a spell. Their search in the cottage led them to a dusty old tome hidden beneath a pile of forgotten books. Its pages crinkled with age, holding secrets of ancient spells and enchantments.

"None of these will work," Margot cried. "Where is mother's book of shadows and light?"

Amelie fetched it at once, her hands trembling as she handed it to her sister. Her fingers had tingled, and that had never happened before.

Margot swung open the book and her fingers traced the faded text, her eyes scanning the words with a mix of curiosity and hope. "I believe I have found something," she whispered. "A spell that could grant us the power to change our appearances."

Amelie's eyes widened with a glimmer of anticipation. "If we can disguise ourselves, we may be able to search for Eloise without drawing attention. It may be the only option to finding her and bringing her back safely."

The sisters wasted no time in preparing for the ritual, gathering the ingredients and creating a sacred space within the cottage. The air crackled with energy as they chanted the ancient incantation, their voices blending together in a harmony of determination. It wasn't as powerful without their sister, but it would have to do.

As the final words left their lips, a shimmering light enveloped Margot and Amelie, their appearances slowly shifting and transforming. They looked at each other, marveling at the uncanny resemblance they now shared. Amelie's straight raven hair had shrunk into tight curls around her face. Her face, previously round and delicate like porcelain, became long and her eyes dark. Margot's fiery red hair straightened into blonde soft waves, with small hints of strawberry. Her freckles faded and the full lips she always loved became very thin.

"We must be careful," Margot warned, her voice sounding strange and unfamiliar even to herself. "We must not let our emotions betray us. We must remain focused on finding Eloise."

With renewed purpose, the sisters ventured out, their disguised forms allowing them to blend into the bustling streets of the town. They moved with caution, eyes scanning the crowd for any sign of Eloise or the treacherous trap that awaited her.

In the center of the square, lifeless bodies were displayed, a grim warning to all who dared to challenge the town's leaders. The sisters' hearts clenched with grief and fury, their disguises unable to conceal the pain etched upon their faces.

Margot's voice quivered with a mix of anguish and determination. "We must not let their sacrifice be in vain. We will find her. The three of us will survive this."

Amelie nodded, her eyes filled with tears that refused to fall. "We will bring justice to those who have taken everything from us. But first, we must find our sister and ensure her safety."

Driven by their grief and the need to protect their remaining family, the sisters pressed forward. Their disguises shielding them from prying eyes as they questioned villagers discreetly. They continued to search for any clues that could lead them to Eloise's whereabouts.

Day turned into night, as the sisters tirelessly searched, their hearts growing heavy with each passing moment. But just as they were losing hope, a familiar face caught Margot's eye—Francois, the younger brother of Louis. He may know something, possibly where Louis was, and she was confident that if she found Louis, she would find her sister.

She followed him discreetly, her heart pounding in her chest. Eventually, he led her to a hidden cellar beneath a dilapidated building. Margot's heart sank as she realized the truth—this was the place where Eloise was being held captive.

Amelie, who had been close behind, joined Margot in the shadows, their shared gaze filled with growing fury. They knew they had to act swiftly, to rescue Eloise.

With a silent understanding, the sisters prepared for the battle that awaited them. They steeled themselves, drawing upon the strength of their bond and the remembrance of their shared purpose. Together, they would face the darkness that threatened to consume their world and reclaim their sister.

As they stepped into the cellar, the sound of their disguised footsteps echoed through the dimly lit room. The time for subtlety had passed; now, it was a fight for their very survival, a fight to protect the love and resilience that bound them together.

Chapter Seven

They ducked into a dark hallway. Margot and Amelie's disguises flickered, their emotions threatening to unravel their carefully woven facade. The important thing was to remain focused. They had to keep their true identities hidden.

As they approached a man guarding the rooms, Margot whispered words of a sleeping spell. Amelie joined her with a harmony and the man snored. Farther down the hallway, Amelie listened intently for the heartbeat of Eloise. When she heard the echo of softer heartbeats, she knew it was Ellie and her unborn child.

Amelie guided them, and they reached the room where Eloise was being held captive. The door creaked open, revealing their sister, her eyes filled with fear, then relief. Eloise, recognizing her sisters despite their disguises, embraced them tightly, her tears mingling with their own.

"We're here, Ellie," Margot whispered, her voice filled with both sorrow and determination. "We will protect you, just as our parents would have wanted."

"I'm so sorry," Eloise began to plea. Her sisters quickly hushed her as they untied where she was bound, one wrist to the cell wall.

"Did Louis do this to you?" Margot demanded an answer from her sister.

Louis was once a source of comfort and joy, but now his name cast a shadow of doubt and betrayal. They knew they had to confront this painful truth, to uncover the depths of deception that had torn their family apart. Eloise frantically shaking her head. She did not know how she felt in this moment.

With hesitant words, Amelie broached the subject, her voice soft. "Eloise, we have discovered unsettling information. Louis was involved in the capture and accusation of our mother."

Eloise's eyes widened, disbelief etched upon her face. "No," she whispered, her voice trembling. "It cannot be true. He was always so loving. I cannot fathom that he would betray us in such a way."

Margot's voice was filled with a mix of anger and sorrow. "We have uncovered evidence, Ellie. Witnesses who saw him in the town's company's leaders, conspiring against our mother. We cannot ignore this truth."

Tears welled in Eloise's eyes as she struggled to come to terms with the devastating revelation. "I loved him," she choked out, her voice filled with heartbreak and anger. "How could he betray us? How could he be a part of the cruelty that took our mother away?"

Amelie reached out, her hand finding Eloise's in a gesture of support. "Love can blind us, sister," she whispered. "We must find the strength to face this betrayal. The memory of our mother will guide us."

"Quickly, drink this" Margot whispered, beginning to chant, with Amelie joining in unison. Within minutes, Eloise's soft brown curls had turned into long blond braids that hugged the side of her head.

Eloise had yet to find or speak to Louis. She had been led to her cell during the night and had been left alone that day, while her captors went to pray in church.

With their disguises intact, the sisters made their way back to the town, their hearts heavy with the weight of their discoveries. They sought Louis, their steps quick but careful, longing for truths that needed to be spoken.

In a secluded alleyway, they found him, his face a mask of surprise and guilt as Margot revealed herself first. The air crackled with tension as Eloise trembled with pain and anger. Eloise was next, while Amelie kept a lookout.

"How could you?" Eloise whispered, her voice filled with a mixture of disbelief and heartbreak. "How could you be a part of the lies and betrayal that tore our family apart?"

He hung his head, unable to meet her gaze. "I was weak," he admitted, his voice laced with regret. "They promised me power and protection, and I succumbed to their manipulation. But know this, Eloise—I never stopped loving you."

Eloise's eyes filled with tears, her voice choked with sorrow. "Love should never justify betrayal," she said, her words filled with a newfound strength.

"I should kill you," Margot roared, knowing that her anger for Louis was deeper than his recent betrayal. "I should kill you for breaking Ellie's heart, for helping them capture our mother."

Eloise interrupted Margot, "I'm pregnant Louis. But

we…" she motioned towards her belly. "We… will do this without you."

Louis fell to his knees and begged for forgiveness. Despite Margot's opinions about him, he had been young and stupid when he broke her heart. That was immaturity. But this was fear of his father. He truly loved Eloise. He wanted a family with her and to run away. Now he watched her walk away and out of his life.

Chapter Eight

E loise cried quietly as the sisters pressed on through the dense forest, her heart broken by the weight of her experiences over the last few days. She had escaped the clutches of her captors with the help of her sisters. But as they approached the hidden cottage that had once been their sanctuary, a sense of foreboding gripped them.

Smoke billowed into the sky, darkening the once serene landscape. The cottage that had provided solace and shelter now lay in ruins. Its charred remains a haunting testament to the darkness that had engulfed their lives. The sisters stood frozen, their eyes filled with a mix of shock and disbelief.

"No," Eloise whispered, her voice barely audible, as if afraid to acknowledge the devastation before her. "This cannot be happening. Our refuge, our home, reduced to ashes."

Margot's voice trembled. "We must find the strength to

move forward," she said, her words laced with a fiery resolve. "Our fight is not over, even in the face of this tragedy."

The sisters sifted through the remnants of the cottage, salvaging what little they could. The fire had claimed much, but they clung to the fragments of their past, nurturing a flicker of hope amidst the ashes.

Amidst the charred debris, Eloise's hand brushed against something solid and cool. She pulled it out, her eyes widening with joy and relief. It was a small box, intricately carved, containing her mother's secret jewels—the heirlooms passed down through generations.

Margot's keen eyes spotted a glimmer beneath a pile of ash. She carefully uncovered a vial, its contents still intact. A surge of nostalgia washed over her as she recognized the familiar aroma of her mother's potent potions. They held the power to heal, protect, and guide them through the trials they would face.

As they continued their search, Amelie's fingers brushed against a worn, leather-bound book. She gasped, clutching it to her chest, her heart filled with gratitude. It was their family's book of shadows and light—the repository of their ancestors' wisdom and the key to unlocking their own magical abilities.

With trembling hands, Amelie opened the book, its pages whispering ancient spells and forgotten incantations. The sisters huddled together, their eyes scanning the words that had been passed down through generations, their mother's guidance echoing in their hearts.

"Now, more than ever, we must honor our family's legacy," Margot said, her voice strong. "We will learn from the wisdom of our ancestors."

Amelie nodded, her eyes shining with a renewed sense of purpose. "Our mother's secrets are not lost, but reborn from the ashes. We will wield them wisely and ensure that her legacy lives on."

Eloise, cradling the jewels and potions in her hands, muttered. "With these treasures, we carry the strength of our family. We will use them to protect and empower ourselves as we navigate the challenges ahead."

As they stood amidst the remains of the cottage, the sisters felt hope. Their mother and father were gone physically, but they had armed the sisters with knowledge, guidance, and power.

With the book of shadows and light, the jewels, and the potions in their possession, the sisters forged ahead. They had reclaimed the secrets lost in the fire, and with them, they would carry the legacy of their family into the future.

Chapter Nine

Eloise clutched her abdomen, a sharp pain coursing through her body. Fear gripped her heart as a crimson stain spread across her dress. The joy and hope that had filled her at the prospect of a new life now mingled with the fear of loss. She feared the worst—a miscarriage.

Margot and Amelie rushed to her side, their eyes wide with concern. "Eloise, what's happening?" Margot asked, her voice trembling with worry.

Eloise's voice quivered as she tried to speak. "I...I don't know," she said, her words barely audible. "Something is wrong. Our baby...I fear for our baby."

"Ellie, we must get you to somewhere that you can hide and rest." Amelie began. "The village councilmen will know that we have rescued you and soon they will come for us."

Gritting her teeth through the pain, Eloise did her best to walk. She wanted to collapse into tears. She had lost the love of her life today, the vision of a family she had always imagined. This pregnancy was a surprise, but gave her hope for the future. She hoped that a baby might change Louis' father's mind about their forbidden love. Any hope for that was sliding through her trembling fingertips.

They were moving slowly and Amelie grew more and more concerned for their safety. *Mother, please help us. We don't know what to do.* She pleaded and hoped for a miracle.

Just as panic threatened to consume them, a voice called out from the shadows, cutting through the haze of despair. "Hold on, dear ones. Help is at hand."

The sisters turned, their eyes widening in disbelief. Standing before them were figures they had long believed to be lost—the members of their coven who had fallen in the face of adversity.

Eloise's eyes brimmed with tears as she recognized their faces, her voice barely a whisper. "But...but you were gone. We mourned your loss."

One of the coven members stepped forward, a kind smile on her face. "We never truly left you, dear Ellie. For everyone's safety, we had to flee, and only your mother knew we were alive. We have been watching, waiting for the right moment to reveal ourselves. But word has spread that they executed your mother, and now the threads of fate have brought us back together."

Amelie's voice trembled with a relief and disbelief. "How is this possible? How did you survive?"

The coven member's eyes twinkled with a mysterious glimmer. "We possess powers and knowledge that extend beyond the mortal realm. We used our magic to shield ourselves, to walk the paths of the unseen. We have been working in the shadows, gathering strength and information, all for the day when we could stand by your side once more."

As they spoke, the pain in Eloise's abdomen subsided, replaced by a gentle warmth. The bleeding slowed, and she let out a shaky breath, grateful for the unexpected turn of events.

The coven members surrounded Eloise, their hands glowing with healing energy. They chanted ancient incantations, their voices a soothing melody that resonated with the very essence of life. Together, they wove a protective spell, a shield of love and hope around the unborn child.

Eloise felt a surge of renewed strength and determination. She knew she was not alone in this journey, that her child and her sisters were surrounded by the unwavering support of their once lost coven.

As the healing energy enveloped her, Eloise looked into the eyes of her sisters, gratitude and determination shining in her gaze. "We are not alone," she whispered, her voice filled with newfound strength. "Our coven has returned, and together, we will face whatever challenges lie ahead."

"We must get you as far away from here as possible. Your... *child* is more important than you understand," Isabella whispered to Eloise, with magic flickering in her eyes. She washed the blood from her hands and hugged her gently.

Eloise did not understand how her unborn child could be important, but she trusted these women. They had just saved her from losing her baby. She would trust their reasoning, whatever it may be.

Sophia and Lena, two of Madeleine's closest friends, drew a circle around their camp. Their incantations were powerful and emotional. They called Madeleine's spirit to help aid in their protection. They would hide the camp for the night and they would travel to their new home in the morning.

The coven members gathered in a circle, their faces filled

with both sorrow and strength. They had reunited with their sisters, but the pain of their past losses still weighed heavily upon them. As they sat together around the burning fire, a hawk flew above, circling and finally perched overhead, watching as if it was standing guard.

One by one, the coven members spoke, their voices filled with grief and resilience. They recounted the moments when their lives had been shattered, when the darkness had claimed their loved ones.

Isabella, with tears streaming down her face, spoke of her husband, Pierre, a kind and gentle soul who had been taken from her too soon. He was protecting her when he was ambushed by guards of the king. She had been promised to another and ran away with Pierre to marry. She described the void that had been left behind, the ache in her heart that had never truly healed.

Sophia, her voice filled with a quiet strength, shared the story of her sister, Katherine, a fierce warrior who had been caring for those who hid from the king's cruelty. When the guards came, she fought valiantly but had ultimately fallen in the battle. Sophia spoke of the courage and determination her sister had displayed, and the fire that burned within her own heart to carry on her sister's legacy.

Lena, her voice steady but filled with pain, spoke of her parents, who had been taken from her while she was a child. They had staged it to look like a tragic accident, but she knew they were killed for her capture. Her gifts had been exposed, and the king wanted her for himself. She described the emptiness she had felt, the longing for their love and guidance that had never faded.

As each story unfolded, the sisters listened intently, their hearts connecting with the shared experiences of loss and grief. They understood the depths of pain that had brought them together, and the strength that had emerged from the darkest chapters of their lives.

Eloise, her voice filled with both gratitude and sorrow, spoke after the others had finished sharing their stories. "We carry the weight of our losses, but we also carry their legacies within us. Our loved ones may be gone, but the love and strength they instilled in us remains. We honor them by continuing our fight for justice and creating a better world."

With tears in their eyes, the fire burned bright and magic sprinkled into the air, signaling a miracle was soon to come, and they nodded in agreement. With renewed resolve, they all stood, their hands entwined. They formed a circle of strength, their collective magic pulsating through their intertwined fingers. In that moment, they made a silent vow to carry the memories of their lost family members in their hearts. To let their love and guidance guide them on their journey forward.

The hawk stayed close and stood guard all night. It wasn't until just before dawn that Margot woke to the hawk stirring in the trees.

Chapter Ten

It was half a day's journey to the sacred grove. There, the twelve coven elders gathered, the vibrant energy of nature enveloping them as they sought guidance and direction. The coven was traditionally led by thirteen elders, but the high priestess was gone. Madeleine, their mother, was the high priestess. With her death, there would only be twelve until another was chosen. They knew they had to come together to determine their next steps, to honor her memory and continue their fight.

Eloise stood at the center, her voice filled with sorrow. "We must decide on our course of action, sisters," she said, her gaze sweeping across the faces of her coven. "Our mother's absence leaves a void, but we cannot let it hinder us. We carry her wisdom within us, and together, we can find our way forward."

As the words left her lips, a wave of conflicting emotions washed over the coven. Each member had their own ideas, their own visions of how to proceed. The air crackled with tension as they debated and voiced their opinions, their voices overlapping in a symphony of disagreement.

Amidst the chaos of dissent, Margot, her voice filled with authority, called for silence. "We must remember that a common cause united us," she said. "Our mother taught us the power of unity, and it is that unity that we must strive to maintain."

Lena, her eyes filled with determination, spoke next. "We must first gather information, understand the true extent of the darkness that plagues our land. Only then can we devise a plan to bring about change."

Isabella, her voice tinged with impatience, countered, "We cannot simply gather information while innocent lives are at stake. We must take action immediately, confront those who seek to bring harm."

They continued to voice their differing opinions, their emotions running high. But through the chaos, a realization settled upon them—a truth that their mother had instilled in them.

Eloise begged her sisters for a break. Her growing belly had seemed to double since she learned of her pregnancy. It had been many weeks, but it seemed to exhaust her more than she expected. It was more than exhaustion. Her fear and worry took over.

Tension hung heavy in the air. Eloise, her hand protectively cradling her growing belly, felt the weight of her unborn child's future pressing upon her, both literally and figuratively. The uncertainty of the situation only added to the intensity of the moment.

Margot, her eyes filled with conviction, spoke. "We must take a more aggressive stance," she declared. "The darkness encroaches upon innocent lives, and we have a duty to protect them. Our actions should be swift and decisive."

Amelie, her voice softer but no less resolute, disagreed. "We cannot risk acting without proper knowledge and understanding," she countered. "We must seek wisdom, gather allies, and approach this challenge with a measured approach. Rushing into action without a rational plan will only bring more harm than good."

Eloise, torn between her sisters' opposing viewpoints, felt the weight of responsibility pressing upon her. She longed for guidance, for a sign that would illuminate the path she should follow.

"We cannot let our differences divide us," Sophia said, her voice filled with conviction. "Our strength lies in our diversity, in our ability to come together and find common ground. We must honor Madeleine's legacy by working together. By respecting each other's perspectives and finding a path that encompasses the best of each idea."

The coven fell silent, their eyes meeting in a shared understanding. They knew that she had entrusted them with the responsibility of upholding the values she had instilled in them—values of love, unity, and perseverance.

In that moment, a sense of unity washed over them, binding them together for a shared purpose. They understood they couldn't see her absence as a hindrance, but an opportunity to step into their own power and forge their own path.

Isabella began by hugging each of the other elders and then the daughters of their late high priestess. She combined the energy of their beating hearts and aligned them all in energy. The coven members saw the threads that wove their ideas together. They realized that gathering information and taking immediate action were not mutually exclusive. They would work in tandem, gathering the knowledge needed to make informed decisions and taking strategic action to protect those in need.

Eloise felt a wave of warmth within her. At that moment, a gentle voice resonated within her mind. It was the voice of their mother, the high priestess, speaking from the realm beyond. "Have faith, my dear Eloise," she whispered. "Your child carries a destiny that will shape the world. Trust in their purpose and the path will become clear."

Eloise's heart skipped a beat. She took a deep breath, finding strength in the words of her mother. "My child," she said, her voice filled with a newfound certainty, "they carry a purpose that will change the world. We honor that destiny, but also ensure their safety and well-being."

Margot's eyes widened with frustration. "Are you suggesting we prioritize the child's safety over the greater good?" she challenged.

Eloise met her sister's gaze, unwavering. "I am suggesting we find a balance. We can gather knowledge, build alliances, and take strategic action while also safeguarding the child. Their birth is a symbol of hope, and their presence in this world will bring about the change we seek. We must protect them, nurture them, so they can fulfill their destiny."

Amelie's expression softened as she listened to her sister's words. "Eloise is right," she said, her voice filled with under-standing. "Our mother believed in the power of balance, and we must follow in her footsteps. We can protect the child and fight for justice simultaneously. It is not an either-or situation."

They must find a balance, a way to protect her child and the future bloodline of witches to come. It was the only way they could survive it.

Chapter Eleven

The coven members embarked on a journey through mystical realms and forgotten lands, their quest to find the ingredients for the most powerful spell their bloodlines had ever known. The sisters were determined to change their fate. They sought the ancient wisdom and magic that would unravel the threads woven by destiny. Knowing that if they failed, the future of Eloise's child and all other witches would be in danger.

Eloise, with her growing belly, led the way. Lena, Isabella, Sophia, Margot, and Amelie followed closely behind. They traversed treacherous terrains, facing formidable challenges with unwavering resolve.

Their first destination was the Whispering Woods, a sacred realm said to hold the secrets of the universe. Amidst the ancient trees, they searched for the elusive Dream Blossom, its petals rumored to possess the ability to manipulate fate itself. As they ventured deeper into the woods, whispers of forgotten prophecies echoed through the air, guiding them towards their blossom.

After days of searching, they finally discovered a grove adorned with the ethereal blooms of the Dream Blossom. With reverence, they plucked the delicate petals, their fingers tingling with the raw power they held. The whispers grew louder, urging them onward to the next stage of their journey.

The second ingredient awaited them in the Caverns of Time. The caverns were dark and challenged each, forcing them to relive their worst memories again in their minds with great intensity. Together, they navigated through winding tunnels until they reached the heart of the caverns, where the Hourglass of Eternity stood, its sands holding the secrets of the past, present, and future.

With a steady hand, Sophia turned the hourglass, watching as the sands shimmered and danced. She collected a vial of the enchanted sand, knowing that its essence would infuse their spell with the power to reshape their bloodline's fate.

The last ingredient took them to the peak of Mount Pyrenees, a place closest to the heavens. Here, they sought the Tears of the Divine, a crystalline substance said to possess the ability to mend the very fabric of destiny. As they ascended the treacherous slopes, storms raged around them, testing their determination. But they pressed on, clinging to the hope of Eloise's child.

At the summit, they stood in awe of the breathtaking sight before them—a waterfall of shimmering tears cascading down from the celestial heavens. Eloise reached out, catching droplets in a chalice, her heart swelling with gratitude for the chance to alter their bloodline's story.

With the ingredients gathered, the coven returned to their sacred sanctum, a place brimming with ancient knowledge and arcane symbols. They prepared for the ritual, their hands trembling with so much at risk.

Isabella would guide Eloise, standing firm by her side, preparing to step in if the spell was too much for her growing pregnant body.

Sophia would guide Margot, a silent shadow, to her strength. Sophia knew that Margot was strong enough, but easily worried about the safety of her sisters. Sophia pushed her to stay, confident that the coven would protect them. The spell needed her complete energy.

Lena would guide Amelie, their energy matching and magnifying the intuition throughout the circle.

As the moon reached its zenith, casting a pale glow upon them, the coven members formed a circle, their voices rising in unison. Gathered in a sacred circle, they decided that the three sisters would lead the spell in place of the high priestess. It was Madeleine's blood that flowed through them—Margot, Eloise, and Amelie—began to cast a spell that would protect their future bloodline and grant them the gifts of patience and wisdom.

Each of the sisters placed the rare ingredients within the cauldron and whispered. Their hearts united, they spoke the words of power, their voices blending in harmony, as they called upon the forces of time and connection to weave their magic.

"By the ancient bond that binds us three,
We cast this spell of destiny.
With love and wisdom, we shall decree,
To protect our bloodline's legacy."

They closed their eyes, their minds attuning to the essence of the spell. They envisioned their book of shadows and light, a sacred tome that would connect them and their future descendants, a vessel of knowledge and guidance passed down through generations.

"Through the book, our spirits intertwine,
A conduit of wisdom, a sacred sign.
In our twenties, our powers shall arise,
A destiny revealed, before our eyes."

As they spoke, the surrounding air shimmered, and a faint glow emanated from their hands. They gently placed their palms upon the surface of an ancient spellbook, feeling the energy surge through their fingertips, binding them together as one.

"Time, we beseech you, grant this our blood,
To wait for power, till the twenty-first sun.
In our youth, no power shall be,
Protect them, our children from scrutiny."

The space filled with a gentle breeze, carrying with it a sense of tranquility and ancient knowledge. The sisters felt a connection forming, a bond that would transcend time and space, linking their future bloodline to their present selves.

"By the power of past, present, and future,
We seal this covenant, unbreakable and sure.
May our descendants find strength in our legacy,
Protected and guided through eternity."

A surge of energy pulsed through the group. Eloise and Margot were filled with hope, but Amelie felt strange.
Something was wrong.

Chapter Twelve

She glanced at Lena with concern and immediately thought of Eloise's unborn child. A subtle disruption had woven its way into their incantation. A slight miscalculation in the alignment of their intentions and energies had gone unnoticed, like a hidden thorn in the beauty of a blooming rose.

As the coven concluded their chant, a surge of energy erupted from the center of their circle. The ground trembled beneath their feet, and the air crackled with an unsettling electricity. The spell, meant to bring balance and protection, had backfired, its intended effects distorted.

In a blinding flash, the coven found themselves surrounded by a chaotic whirlwind of elemental forces. The once serene clearing became a stormy battleground, with gusts of wind tearing at their hair and robes, flames dancing uncontrollably, and the very earth beneath them trembling with an unseen force.

Fear and confusion consumed the coven as they desperately struggled to regain control. Their voices rose in a chorus of counter-incantations, attempting to redirect the unleashed energies. But their efforts seemed futile, for the magic had taken on a life of its own, refusing to be tamed.

With the storm intensifying, the coven realized the dire consequences of their spell. They had disrupted the very balance they sought to restore, and the realm they had hoped to protect was now faced with uncertainty.

In an ultimate act of desperation, Isabella stepped forward, shielding Eloise, her voice trembling. She channeled the remnants of their collective power, focusing her will on containing the tempest. With a surge of energy, she created a shield, encapsulating the coven within its protective embrace.

As the storm raged on outside the shield, the coven huddled together, their hearts heavy with the weight of their unintended consequences.

In the spell's aftermath, the coven realized the true lesson of their misfortune—the delicate balance of magic, the importance of respect and mindfulness in their craft, and the necessity of accepting the consequences of their actions.

Strange occurrences plagued the sisters' lives. Objects levitated without warning. The weather shifted as their moods and dreams became vivid and prophetic.

Confusion and concern settled upon the sisters. They had cast the spell with the best intentions, but it seemed to have backfired. They were unsure of how.

Seeking answers, they gathered, calling upon the spirits of their mother and father, but they did not come. Eloise, her hand protectively resting on her growing belly, felt a responsibility for her unborn child and the future of their bloodline.

"We must understand what went wrong," Margot said.

"We thought we had protected our bloodline, but something went wrong."

Amelie nodded in agreement, her brow furrowed with worry. "We must bring balance back to our lives and ensure that our future descendants do not suffer the consequences of our actions."

Days turned into nights as they consulted with the ethereal presence of their ancestors. Together, they unraveled the mystery, discovering a long-forgotten passage that was overlooked during their initial research.

"The spell of protection," Eloise read aloud, her voice once again trembling with remorse. "It states that in rare cases, the power of the coven's intent can amplify their powers. It seems we unwittingly tapped into an unforeseen reservoir of energy."

The sisters exchanged glances, a mix of guilt and determination reflected in their eyes. They knew they had to regain control over their powers and protect their future bloodline.

Eloise, her voice filled with conviction. "We must learn to harness and control our powers, to bring them into balance. Only then can we ensure the safety of this baby and our future descendants."

Margot nodded. She hid the fear behind her confidence. She wouldn't allow her sisters to see her worry. *Mother, we need you.*

A faint glow that started between the sisters grew, its energy bright and forceful. It extended out towards the forest in a never ending blinding light. The air shimmered, and a familiar presence filled their space.

It was the spirit of their mother, the high priestess from beyond the realms of the living.

Margot, Eloise, and Amelie turned towards the ethereal figure, their hearts filled with longing and gratitude. Their mother's spirit emanated a warm and comforting energy, a beacon of wisdom and love.

"Mother," Eloise whispered, her voice choked with emotion. "We have missed you."

The spirit of their mother smiled, her eyes filled with a gentle understanding. "My dear daughters, I have never truly left your side. I am here to guide you and offer the wisdom of our bloodline. But there is something I must show you first."

Eloise, with her hand protectively resting on her growing belly, felt a calming hope. "Mother, we seek to understand. Please show us the way?"

The spirit nodded and gestured for the sisters to join hands. As they closed their eyes, they felt a shift in the atmosphere, as if they were being transported to another time and place. When they opened their eyes, they found themselves in a hazy memory, observing their mother as a young woman.

They watched as their mother, radiant and full of life, conversed with a young man. Gasping with surprise, they recognized him. It was Louis and Francois' father, Philippe, a suitor who had once sought her hand in marriage. The same man that Margot and Amelie saw in the clearing. He was smiling, a side of him no one knew existed. He was clearly in love with their mother, and she loved him in return.

The memories moved to her childhood home, where Philippe asked for her hand in marriage from her father.

"You are not good enough for our Madeleine. You cannot give her what she needs. You should be ashamed, coming here with nothing to offer our daughter but your love. That is not enough." Antoine answered with a cruel laugh.

Philippe's expression shifted from disappointment to anger. He transformed from a young man in love to one with a vengeful heart.

The memory faded, and the sisters found themselves back in the present. Eloise wiped away tears, her heart heavy with a mix of emotions.

"How could our papa do that to you, mother? You clearly loved him." Amelie cried.

"Philippe refused to see me after that day. I did not know the truth until papa was on his deathbed. By then, I had moved on and met your father. It was too late to make amends. Philippe would never change his mind about our family. The very reason he forbid you to love his son," Madeleine explained. "My love is with you always. But like some mistakes, some spells cannot be mended."

The girls joined, hoping to understand the magnitude of their miscalculations.

"It is true, the youth of our bloodline will no longer have powers until they are twenty-one. Our family book of shadows and light will no longer exist. Each descendant will receive their book on their twenty-first birthday. It will depend on the surrounding elders to guide them on their journey. Take care of each other. Philippe will not stop looking for you." Madeleine warned. As her spirit faded, the sisters embraced each other in tears.

Chapter Thirteen

The sisters, Margot, Eloise, and Amelie, gathered, with the weight of the consequences they had faced. They now understood where Philippe's hate for their family had begun. After much contemplation, they reached a collective decision - it was time to seek a new location, far away from their current surroundings, in order to ensure their safety.

Eloise, her hand protectively resting on her belly. "I fear my child is coming soon, much too soon than should be."

"Everything will be fine. My heart has been full of worry lately, but your child does not bring that worry. I feel sure that your child and the prophecy will be fulfilled.

Margot nodded, her expression resolute. "By relocating to a new place, we can establish a fresh start, away from the prying eyes and potential threats that may arise. We must get away from Philippe"

Amelie, her voice filled with determination, added, "We

must find a location where we can freely explore and control our magic, without endangering those around us. It is our duty to ensure the safety of our loved ones."

"It is decided then, we leave in the morning. We shall say our goodbyes to the rest of the coven tonight, but we will not tell them where we are going." Margot confirmed, "They will understand."

A shriek left Eloise's lips, and both Margot and Amelie were at her side at once, catching her as she collapsed onto the ground. "The baby is coming." Eloise screamed.

Before they could respond, Sophia, Lena and Isabella were at the door, ready to help. "There is a spell for birth." Isabella explained. "Your mother taught it to us, and we have helped many women birth children."

Eloise nodded in a silent plea to her sisters and the elders. Isabella began. "In the mystical realm of the written word, I shall conjure a spell to ease Eloise in the delivery of her baby. With love and care, let the incantation begin:

On this sacred day, as life prepares to unfold,
I summon the power of ancient magic, wise and bold.
With every word I speak, let the pain subside,
As Eloise's journey to motherhood we will guide.

From the depths of the earth, I draw strength and grace,
To embrace Eloise's body and create a tranquil space.
With each breath she takes, let her fears melt away,
As the magic of this spell brings comfort and allay.

Gentle winds, blow softly, soothe her weary soul,
Whisper words of reassurance, let tranquility take control.
Let the moon's gentle glow illuminate the room,
Radiating calmness, dispelling any gloom.

The waters of life, pure and serene,
Flow through Eloise, serene and pristine.
With each surge, let her body find release,
As the pain transforms into a sense of peace.

The flickering flames of the sacred fire,
Wrap Eloise in warmth, lifting her higher.
Ignite within her strength and resilience,
As the magic of this spell aids her deliverance.

Guiding spirits of ancient lineage and might,
Descend upon this space, bringing comfort and light.
Wrap your loving embrace around Eloise's form,
Empowering her, keeping her safe and warm.

As the spell unfolds, let the pain fade away,
Replacing it with joy and serenity, I pray.
May Eloise's birthing journey be one of bliss,

By the power of the elements, by the strength of our bond,
May Eloise find peace and strength to respond.
This spell is cast with love and great care,
To ease her pain and help her baby safely share.

As I seal this spell with intentions pure and true,
May Eloise's delivery be gentle and smooth, too.
Blessed be this moment, blessed be this day,
As new life enters the world in a magical way.

So mote it be.

With the completion of this spell, may Eloise find solace and comfort, and may her delivery be eased and filled with love."

As the labor intensified, Eloise's strength and determination shone through. She drew upon the power of her lineage, channeling the ancient wisdom of her ancestors for support. The sisters remained steadfast in their love and encouragement, providing comfort with every breath.

Sophia and Lena kept Eloise comfortable and encouraged. While Isabella monitored the baby and prepared for its arrival.

Hours passed, and as the baby emerged into the world, a

profound silence fell upon the room. But then, to the astonishment of everyone present, another baby followed, and then another. Eloise had given birth to not one, but three healthy infant girls. Isabella exchanged glances with Lena and Sophia, smiling with pride.

"Your mother was right and she would be so proud." Isabella whispered.

Tears of joy streamed down Eloise's face as she held her precious bundles in her arms. The sisters exchanged amazed glances, marveling at the unexpected gift given to them. The space seemed to shimmer with delight, as if celebrating these three extraordinary beings.

Eloise gazed down at her newborns, feeling love and awe. "Threefold blessings," she whispered, her voice filled with wonder. "We bless our bloodline with three souls, each destined for greatness."

Margot and Amelie, their hearts overflowing with gratitude, nodded in agreement. "They are a testament to the strength and resilience of our bloodline," Margot said, her voice filled with pride.

Amelie added, "These three souls shall carry our legacy forward, united in their bond."

As the sisters reveled in the joyous moment, a sense of purpose settled upon them. They knew that their newfound family was a symbol of hope.

The surrounding woods seemed to hum with anticipation. As if acknowledging the significance of this extraordinary birth. The sisters named the children together—Aria, Seraphina, and Madeleine. Each name carrying the weight of their bloodline's history and the promise of a bright future.

With the arrival of the triplets, the sisters' unity grew stronger, their bond fortified by the shared responsibility of raising these extraordinary beings. They knew their journey was far from over, and that the challenges they faced would only deepen their connection. Word had spread that Philippe was adding more resources to find them.

As they cradled the newborns in their arms, the sisters sat together, their hearts heavy. They recognized that separating the triplets would be a painful sacrifice, but they also understood that it was necessary.

Eloise spoke first. "It is time for us to embrace our motherhood as sisters and allow these children to thrive under our individual guidance."

With heavy hearts, the sisters reached a consensus. Eloise would take Seraphina, Margot would take Aria, and Amelie would take Madeleine. Each child would grow up separately, and they would reunite on their twenty-first birthday. Each sister would raise a child as their own.

When word spread to the coven, Isabella, Lena and Sophia offered themselves to help each of the sisters. They insisted that the girls not be alone, but understood the importance of separation.

The day of separation arrived, emotions running high as the sisters bid farewell to each other. Aria, Seraphina, and Madeleine, though young, sensed the significance of the moment.

Eloise looked into Seraphina's eyes, her voice filled with love, "You are my daughter, Seraphina, and I will guide you through life's journey with all the love and wisdom that flows through our bloodline. With Isabella, we will travel to Lancashire."

Margot held Aria close, her voice steady, "Aria, my dear, you carry the spark of our magic within you. I will nurture that flame and help you unleash your true potential. With Lena, we will travel far to the rocky shores of Ireland."

Amelie embraced Madeleine, her voice filled with determination, "Madeleine, my daughter, you possess a strength and resilience that will shape the world. I will be there, every step of the way, to guide you on your path. With Sophia, we are traveling to Sicily."

With tearful goodbyes, the sisters parted ways, each taking their child and embarking on a new chapter of their lives. Though physically separated, the sisters remained connected through their bloodline, their shared experiences, and the bond forged through sisterhood. For the next twenty-one years they would hide from Philippe.

About the Author

Born in Southeast Asia and raised Hawaii, Selene fell in love with stories. English wasn't her first language, but soon after her mother passed away, it would be the only language she spoke.

Writing and story telling would become a tool for Selene to cope with the challenges of life around her. After high school, she moved to the mainland and began her search for her truest self.

She loves a good romance but is also a huge fan of epic fantasy and most things paranormal; if there are vampires, werewolves, shifters, fae, elves, dragons or witches… count her in!

A wife, mother of two kids and two fur-babies, she juggles her time between working, school, family activities and a social life. Her favorite time to write is anytime, that the rest of the house is still sleeping, always working on the next story to share.

I hope you enjoyed *Covens and Curses*, my debut novella.
Covens and Curses is the prequel for the series;
NOT ALL WITCHES LIVE IN SALEM